THORFINN
NICEST VIKING

For Daniel – D.M.

To Viking Isobel, the Fish Gobbler – R.M.

Young Kelpies is an imprint of Floris Books
First published in 2016 by Floris Books

The publisher acknowledges subsidy from Creative Scotland towards the publication of this volume

British Library CIP data available
ISBN 978-178250-233-3
Printed in Great Britain
by Bell & Bain Ltd

Thorfinn and the Raging Raiders

written by David MacPhail
illustrated by Richard Morgan

HARALD THE SKULL-SPLITTER
CHIEF OF INDGAR
THORFINN THE
VERY-VERY-NICE-INDEED
FREYA
WILFRED THE
SPLEEN-MINCER

OSWALD
WISE MAN OF INDGAR
VELDA
SVEN THE
HEAD-CRUSHER
HAGAR THE
BRAIN-EATER

ELK POLO PITCH
INDGAR VILLAGE
COW SHEDS

OSWALD'S HOUSE
THE GREAT HALL
THORFINN'S HOUSE
MARKET PLACE

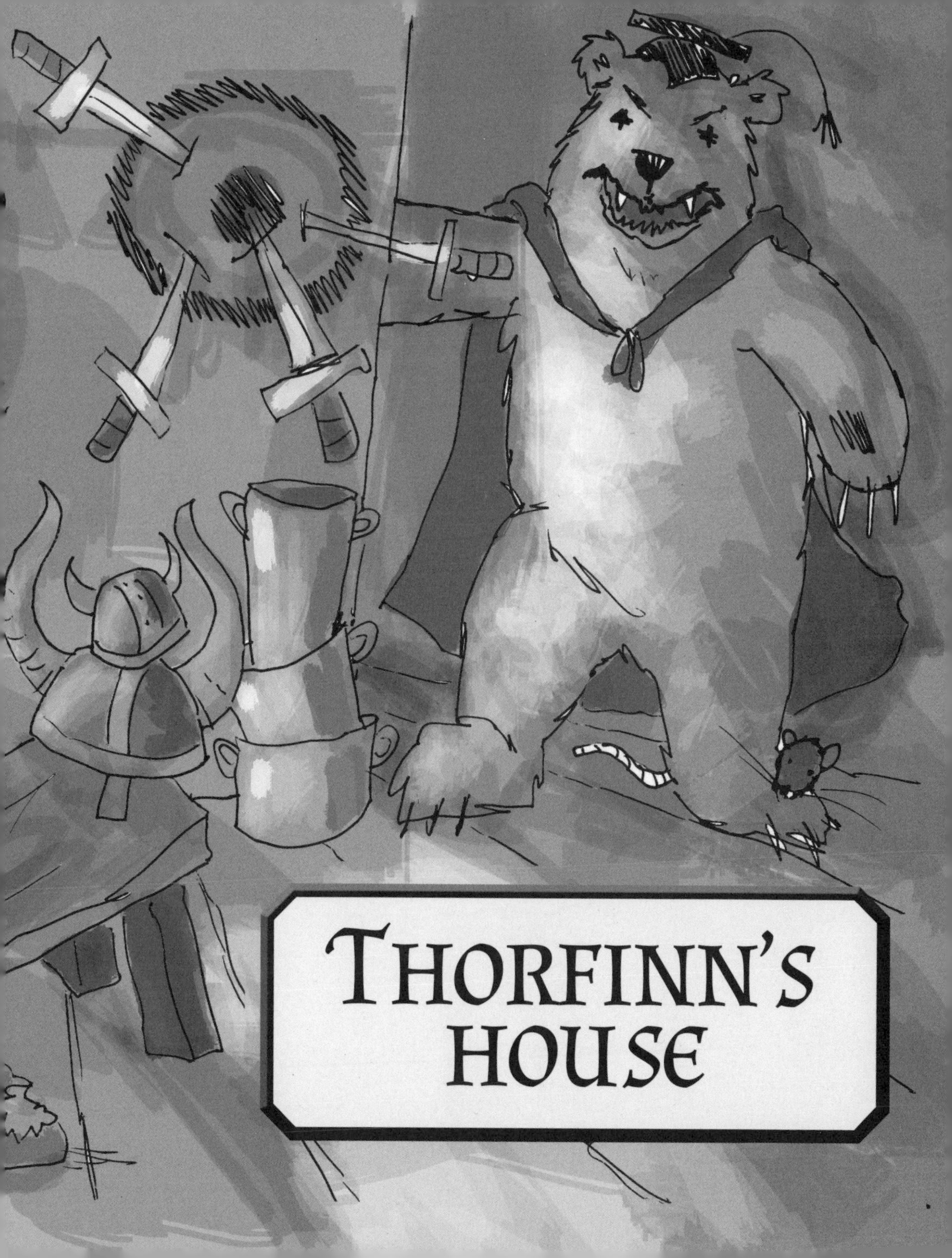
THORFINN'S
HOUSE

"BREAKFAAAAAASSSSSST!"

CHAPTER 1

Breakfast time in any Viking house was a messy business, but in the house of Harald the Skull-Splitter, the famous Viking chief, it was complete chaos. It was a bit like a chimpanzees' tea party. The big daddy of all chimpanzees' tea parties, in fact, where the chimpanzees were three times bigger and seven times more quarrelsome.

The house was a whirlwind of flying furniture, flying food and flying fists. Harald's three eldest sons were having a wrestling match in the middle of the kitchen floor.

The eldest was Wilfred the Spleen-Mincer, who'd just got back from a gap year invading Russia.

Next there was Sven the Head-Crusher, who'd been away at Viking university. His special subjects were kidnapping and ransom.

And finally Hagar the Brain-Eater, who'd spent the last year tracking and hunting polar bears in the frozen north because, as he put it, "One of them looked at me funny."

"Take that, chicken brain!" cried Wilfred, hoisting a heavy sideboard into the air and launching it in Sven's direction.

"RRRAAAAARRR!" roared Sven as he dodged the sideboard, snatched a fallen vase from the floor and smashed it over Hagar's head.

"GRRRRR!" growled Hagar, shaking bits of vase out of his hair before grabbing a chair in both hands and breaking it over Wilfred's back.

The three boys looked a lot like their father, except Harald's beard was bigger and bushier, of course. He'd won the award for Viking Beard of the Year four times in a row.

"Ha! That's my boys," said Harald, beaming proudly and beating his mighty fist on the table.

Beside Harald, at the centre of this whirlwind, sat his youngest son, whose Viking name was rather different from the others: Thorfinn the Very-Very-Nice-Indeed.

Thorfinn stood up, a kind smile spreading across his face, and raised his helmet to his father.

"Good morning to you, dear Dad." He was the exact opposite of Harald's other sons. He was the nicest, most polite Viking who had ever lived.

Thorfinn sat back down and admired his carefully placed eggcup, knife, spoon and neatly folded napkin. He calmly cut his toast into soldiers and sipped pinecone tea, totally unruffled by the chaos going on around him. In fact he was humming. "Hmm, hmm, hmm... hmm. Dum-de-dum..."

Thorfinn's pet pigeon, Percy, a lovely speckled bird, was perched on the table beside him, cheerfully pecking up a few leftover crumbs.

The three older boys grappled with each other in the middle of the floor and crashed into the breakfast table, catapulting Thorfinn's egg across the kitchen.

SPLATTT!

"ENNOUGHH!" screamed another voice, the fearsome, high-pitched cry of a Viking woman.

CHAPTER 2

Thorfinn's mother, Freya, emerged from the tangle of bodies with one brother in a headlock, one in an earlock, and the other sandwiched between her knees. Her long blonde hair cascaded over a set of piercing green eyes.

"This is the fourth time this week you lot have wrecked this kitchen. Now sit down and eat your breakfast nicely, like Thorfinn."

The three brothers suddenly looked sheepish, and they meekly sat down at the table.

Thorfinn raised his helmet again and saluted them. "Good morning, Wilfred. Good morning, Sven. Good morning, Hagar. And what a lovely day it is!"

Thorfinn's brothers just growled at him.

"By Thor, that was a good contest!" cried Harald in his deep, booming voice. Then he started dishing out fighting tips to his three eldest sons. "Sven, you need to get tighter on your opponent. Hagar, you must work on your sidestep. Wilfred, you're too slow in attack."

Freya doled out bowls of steaming hot porridge to each of them. Thorfinn savoured every mouthful then dabbed at the side of his mouth with a napkin.

Wilfred, Sven and Hagar slurped the porridge down in one go, chucked their bowls onto the floor behind them and burped:

They were long, mighty burps that ran together, sounding like the call of a giant sea monster.

Freya groaned angrily. "I am SICK of clearing up after you layabouts. It's not my job, you know, just because I'm your mother. The only one who helps is Thorfinn."

"Mother is right," said Thorfinn. "We should all take turns at doing the housework. I can draw up a rota if you like."

Thorfinn's brothers burst into peals of laughter, as did Harald. Great, thundering, thigh-slapping laughter that shook the dust off the rafters.

"HA! Housework!" bellowed Sven.

"What will you think up next?" said Hagar, walloping Thorfinn on the shoulders.

"You and that daft pigeon!" said Wilfred, shaking his head.

"Ah, don't laugh at Thorfinn," replied Harald. "Remember, Thorfinn is the cleverest of us all. He and his pigeon have saved this village many times. But then again... HOUSEWORK?! Vikings don't do housework!"

Once he'd finished laughing, Harald spat what remained of his food onto the floor and leapt to his feet. "Right, if you lads want to see some REAL wrestling, follow me!"

"HUZZAH!" cried Thorfinn's brothers, and Harald led them charging through the house, kicking down the front door in the usual Viking way.

CHAPTER 3

"Grrr... that's the sixth front door they've wrecked this month!" Thorfinn's mother yanked open a drawer full of woodworking tools and strapped on a pair of goggles. "My work is NEVER done!" She sighed, and dragged a workbench out of the cupboard.

"Please, dear Mother, allow me to me help," said Thorfinn.

But she wasn't listening. She was too busy taking her frustration out on a piece of wood. She was sawing so hard, she was engulfed in a cloud of sawdust.

After they'd finished repairing the front door, tidying the kitchen and cleaning up the breakfast dishes, Freya slumped down at the kitchen table. Thorfinn made her a cup of pinecone tea and Percy dragged over a biscuit in his beak.

"I'm so fed up, Thorfinn," she said. "What would I do without your help?"

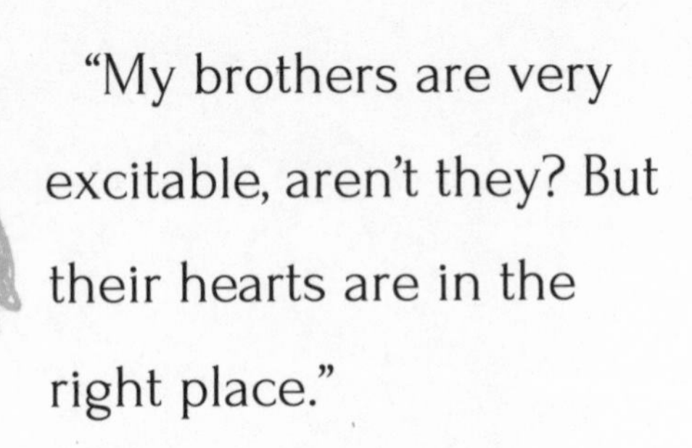

"My brothers are very excitable, aren't they? But their hearts are in the right place."

"You are always so forgiving, dear Thorfinn. But I really am fed up. Since the three of them came home, the house has been chaos. Last night, Wilfred and Hagar dressed up as bears and had a battle in the living room. There are bite marks all over the place and I'm sure one of them actually ate the sheepskin rug. And Sven kidnapped next-door's cow and locked it in the barn. He said it was his homework."

She flicked open a copy of the local news

parchment, *The Daily Hatchet*. There was an advert on the back page along with a map of Iceland:

SPA BREAKS IN ICELAND!

VIKINGS!

Are you sick of pillaging?
Do you want a break from the same old humdrum routine of sailing about and burning villages to the ground?

COME TO FLOTTERHEIM ICELANDIC SPA!
Enjoy the hot waters of the volcano! Take off your helmet! Put down your sword for a bit and relax!

“That looks wonderful, Mother. You should go,” said Thorfinn.

“I’d love to go on holiday, but who would look after this place?” she said.

“I’d be very happy to look after things while you’re away,” said Thorfinn.

Freya smiled. “Thank you, Thorfinn, but it wouldn’t be fair to leave all this to you. You’re the youngest and littlest in the family. Besides, they should be able to look after themselves.”

“If you say so, Mother, but you deserve a nice relaxing break. If you change your mind, I will do all I can to help.” Thorfinn tapped his shoulder and Percy hopped onto it. He picked up his school bag and lifted his helmet. “I bid you good day, dear Mother.”

"And good day to you, my darling boy." She kissed him on the cheek then turned and dragged a giant basket of fresh laundry into the kitchen. She pulled out an enormous pair of elk-skin underpants, which, judging by their size, belonged either to Harald or to a large-buttocked rhinoceros.

CHAPTER 4

Thorfinn's best friend, Velda, was waiting for him outside. "Good morning, Mrs Skull-Splitter!" she called in to Freya, who was too busy to reply.

Velda was as fearsome as she was skinny, and her enormous helmet wobbled around on her tiny head. Normally she carried a giant axe, but today she was practising her swing with a polo stick, because they had an elk-polo match later that morning.

"What's wrong, Thorfinn?" she asked, as they headed out of the village of Indgar, through the forest and up the hill, with Percy fluttering from branch to branch above. "Don't tell me your brothers wrecked the house again?"

"I'm afraid they did, old pal."

"I bet your mum's pretty angry. I don't know how she puts up with it."

"I've never seen her so fed up," said Thorfinn. "I'm not sure what to do."

"Hmmm..." Velda drummed her fingers on her chin. "I could wallop them – your brothers, I mean – with my polo stick. Do you want me to wallop them for you?"

"Many thanks for the offer," replied Thorfinn. "I always appreciate your advice. But I'm not sure walloping them is the answer."

Velda shrugged. "It always works for me." She swung her polo stick and belted a rock into the sky.

"Perhaps Oswald will know what to do," said Thorfinn.

Oswald was an incredibly old man with an incredibly long beard and an incredibly loud and whiny voice. He was the village wise man and he lived in a hut in the woods.

Oswald ran the village school, which had just

two pupils – Thorfinn and Velda. For most Vikings, school was simply a way of ruining a perfectly good day's sword fighting, spear fighting, fist fighting or any other sort of fighting.

Velda would also rather be out fighting. She only went to school because Thorfinn's father had made her promise to keep Thorfinn out of trouble; that, and Oswald's free homemade pancakes.

"Now then," said Oswald, pouring out pinecone tea, "we're studying geography today."

Velda groaned. "I HATE geography!"

"You say that about every subject we do, which is a great pity," said Oswald, "because you can learn a lot at school. This, for example..." Oswald pulled out a string with a small metal fish dangling on the end.

An 'N' was carved into its nose, an 'S' on its tail, and an 'E' and a 'W' on each side. "Do you know what this is?"

Thorfinn's eyes brightened. "It's a compass, isn't it?"

"It is indeed," said Oswald. "It's magnetic, so the fish's nose always points north."

"So what?" said Velda. "North is cold, south is hot, west is the sea, and the east is not – what else is there to know?"

"Ah, but say, for example, your longship is stuck in fog in the middle of the sea. The compass tells you exactly which direction is which."

"My father had a compass," said Velda. Her shoulders slumped. "Fat lot of good it did him."

Velda's father, Gunga the Navigator, was one of the worst navigators in Viking history. He had set off one day in search of the New World and had never been seen again.

Oswald raised his eyebrows and handed the fish to Thorfinn. "There, that's for you to practise with. And this..." He plucked a small brown cylinder from his robe and passed it to Thorfinn too. "This is a spyglass. If you look at things through it, they appear closer than they are, which can be useful at sea."

"How interesting! Thanks, old friend," said Thorfinn. "And do you have any suggestions for how I can help my mother, now that my brothers are home?"

"Hmmm..." Oswald scratched his head for a moment. He was so deep in thought, he dropped the pancake he'd been holding on the floor and trod on it. The jam and cream splurged out from under his sandal. He didn't even notice. "The lot of Viking mothers is a tricky one. They're expected to be as tough as men – to wrestle with elks and tame wolves. Yet at the same time they must care for their children, look after their husbands, hunt and cook the food, clean the house, make the clothes—"

"All the rubbish stuff!" declared Velda through a mouthful of pancake. "It's not fair! Why are women expected to do all that?" She turned to Thorfinn, fuming. "Are you sure you don't want me to wallop your brothers?"

Thorfinn politely shook his head. "I quite agree with you, though: it isn't fair. We should share the household tasks. It shouldn't all be down to poor Mother."

"You'll have a problem persuading your father and brothers," said Oswald. "If you ask a Viking man to do housework he'll laugh at you – if you're lucky. He might also lop your head off."

"I did ask," said Thorfinn. "And they did laugh."

"Pretty please can I wallop them?" said Velda.

"No, dear pal," said Thorfinn. "I'll find another way. Come on, we'll be late for our elk-polo match."

"Hmmm..." said Oswald, rubbing his chin again. He looked around. "Now, where did I put that pancake of mine?"

CHAPTER 5

Elk polo was by far the most popular sport in Indgar village, and there was a big match at least once a month.

Indgar's polo pitch was on a meadow just above the village. Practically the entire population was at the match that afternoon, crammed into big stands around the sides of the pitch – except those poor people, like Thorfinn's mum, who were too busy tidying up the other Vikings' mess.

The crowd erupted as the two teams, one in red and one in blue, rode out onto the pitch. Most of the crowd were waving blue flags.

"COME ON YE BLUUUUUES!" they chanted.

Thorfinn's team, the reds, mostly consisted of children and the elderly. Thorfinn led them out, riding his favourite elk, Marjory. Marjory didn't like getting her feet wet, so she tiptoed round all the muddy puddles, which made it look like she was doing a funny dance.

"That'a girl, Marjory," said Thorfinn, patting her neck.

This brought gales of laughter from the crowd. "Look at Thorfinn! Him and his daft elk are doing the foxtrot!"

Velda followed Thorfinn, riding her elk, Thunder. Thunder was red-eyed, ferocious and frothing at the mouth. As was Velda.

"GRRRRR... I can't wait to get stuck into them!" she yelled.

Next came Oswald, who was half asleep on an equally elderly and dozy elk called Gladys.

The blue team, however, included some of the meanest and biggest Vikings of Indgar. Some of them were even larger than the elks they were riding. They were like a team of bellowing bulls.

They were led by Harald's second in command, Erik the Ear-Masher, who was almost as wild and ferocious as the village chief himself. He glared at

Thorfinn with wicked glee. "It's payback time for all that horrible politeness!"

Behind him rode his son, Olaf, a large boy with a face like a mangled turnip. He was rubbing his hands together. "Oh boy, justice at last!"

Harald watched from the sidelines, along with Thorfinn's three brothers.

"Ach! This is going to be rubbish!" said Sven.

"The blue team will rip Thorfinn's team apart," said Wilfred. "It will be the shortest match ever."

"We'll be picking up pieces of Thorfinn from the grass," laughed Hagar. The three brothers waved their blue flags in the air.

"COME ON YE BLUES!"

"I wouldn't be so sure," said Harald, snatching

up a red flag and waving it. "Thorfinn's clever, and he's fast."

The whistle blew and the game kicked off.

"COME ON THE REDS!" Velda screamed like a Valkyrie, and charged into battle.

CHAPTER 6

Have you ever seen a mouse tackle a pride of lions? That's exactly what it was like watching Velda playing elk polo. She leapt onto the back of one of the enormous blues and wrestled the reins from him. Then she steered his panicking elk towards another two blue players. She jumped off just before they collided and rolled to her feet.

“Hmm,” said Thorfinn. “I’m not sure the rules allow such a move.”

The blue team’s entire front row collapsed in a huge pile, like a set of elk-and-Viking dominoes.

“There’s nothing in the rule book that says I can’t jump on top of another player,” yelled Velda.

“Hmm... fair point,” said Thorfinn.

Velda’s unusual tactic of wiping out the blue team’s forwards caused a huge fist fight, with Velda at its centre. The Vikings loved nothing more than a good old punch-up. The Viking spectators poured out of the stands, some of them to get a better look, some of them to join in. Before long everyone was involved. The pitch turned into one giant scrum of flying fists, flying bodies, flying polo

sticks and even flying elks.

Everyone, that is, except Oswald and Gladys, who were now fast asleep, and Thorfinn, Marjory and Percy, who sat on the sidelines watching.

Percy perched on Marjory's head and raised his wing as if to say something.

"Yes indeed, old pal," said Thorfinn to the bird. "My fellow Vikings are a strange bunch."

"ZZZZZZZZ," Oswald snored.

Then suddenly the air was filled with a deafening blaring noise.

"HHHHHHONNNNNNNNKKKK!"

Rodrik the Big-Eyed, who was the village lookout, appeared on the crest of the hill, holding his giant horn.

"STOOOOOOPPPPPPPPP!"

He also had a loud, bellowing voice.

The fight stopped abruptly, and Harald emerged from the middle of the crowd carrying two men in headlocks. "What is it, Rodrik? What's the matter?"

Rodrik pointed down the hillside.

"ATTTTTAAAAAAAAACKKKK!"

CHAPTER 7

Harald looked down the hill to see a number of strange longships gathered on the shore. They were Viking ships, no doubt, but their sails were unfamiliar. A pall of black smoke was rising from Indgar's great hall.

Harald gasped. "RAIDERS!"

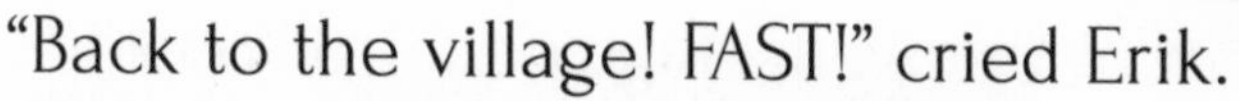

"Back to the village! FAST!" cried Erik.

Everyone raced down the hill, but by the time they reached the shore the raiders had already cast off and were sailing down the fjord.

The village was a mess. Houses had been ransacked and wagons overturned. Cattle sheds had been broken into and there were cows and chickens running around everywhere.

Harald darted to and fro, shouting orders to the villagers. "Round up the cattle! Put out that fire!"

Thorfinn and Oswald noticed some graffiti daubed on one of the walls. Big red letters read:

“Hmm... how rude,” said Thorfinn.

“Mmmm...” said Oswald the wise man, scratching his chin. “What peculiar things for a ferocious Viking raider to write.”

It soon turned out that the fire was much smaller than expected. In fact, the smoke wasn’t coming from the great hall but something in front of it.

“They burned our underpants!” cried Erik the Ear-Masher. “All the underpants in the village!” They’d just been washed and were hanging out on a line in the marketplace.

There was a horrified glare in Harald's eyes. "What kind of sick, twisted person would burn another Viking's underpants!?"

Soon, the last wagon was righted and the last animal was returned to its pen.

"You know," said Thorfinn, gazing up at the single remaining pair of underpants in the whole village, which the raiders had left flying, flag-like, from the roof of the great hall, "they didn't actually do much damage. I'm beginning to think this was some kind of practical joke."

"You always think the best of people, Thorfinn," said Oswald.

"Huh! They just didn't get the chance," said Velda. "They must have seen us coming and legged it. Lucky for them."

Harald stared out to sea, his face purple, his eye twitching with rage. Harald's eye always twitched when he was angry. "GRRR!"

Erik the Ear-Masher joined him, as did Velda and the others. They were all fuming. Vikings spent their whole lives raiding and pillaging other people's villages. They were mortally offended when someone raided theirs.

Thorfinn flipped open a pouch on his belt and pulled out the spyglass Oswald had given him. He pointed at the departing longships. The first thing he saw was a man's face, big and bulgy, with a red nose

and ginger hair. He was hanging over the stern, looking back towards Indgar, blowing raspberries at them.

"How vulgar," said Thorfinn.

"What's that you've got?" asked Erik.

"It lets me see faraway things up close. Look."

He offered the spyglass to Erik, who peered through it. "Oh yes! Look at their sails. They'll be easy to find. There's a giant skull on the main sail, with a Viking helmet and crossed axes."

At that moment Thorfinn's three brothers came tearing out of the woods from the direction of the house, like a pack of charging elephants. "DAD! The raiders have taken Mum!"

"WHAT?!" cried Harald.

"They've kidnapped her," said Wilfred. "So Sven says."

"Yeh," said Sven. "They're probably going to ransom her and demand all your gold. I did a module on it at university."

Hagar scoffed at his brother. "Always going on about ST-UUUU-PID university."

"Huh! You can talk," Sven scoffed right back, "Mr 'I wrestle polar bears' – NOT!"

The two brothers jostled each other and almost came to blows, but Harald stopped them with a mighty roar:

"SHUUTTT UUUUUUUUPPP!"

At the sound of this, a frail old man popped his head out from a barrel of pickled herring. It was Ergil the Wood-Whittler, who usually sat in the square all day carving.

"Help! Please! I'm stuck! They stuffed me in this barrel of stinking fish, the swines!"

"Did you see my wife?" barked Harald.

"Yes, I saw your wife struggling with them. They dragged her down to the boats."

Harald was like a geyser about to erupt. "They dared to kidnap my wife? MY wife? RAAAR!" He grabbed an axe and launched it in the direction of the raiders' ships. It didn't get anywhere near the ships, of course, but it did scatter a flock of seagulls, and it nearly knocked out a poor seal that had just popped its head out of the water.

"By Odin, I will make them pay." Harald jumped up onto the barrel of herring, forcing Ergil back down into the fishy goo, and yelled, "EVERYONE, TO THE SHIPS!"

The villagers roared, "LET'S GET THEM!" and they raced to the pier.

A soggy head popped up from the barrel again. "Wait!" Ergil called after them. "Is nobody going to pull me out?"

CHAPTER 8

"ME FIRST!"

"NO, ME!"

The entire population of Indgar raced to the boats, barging past each other to join the pursuit.

"I'll make mincemeat out of them!" cried one.

"PAH!" cried another. "I'll make mincemeat, then turn it into sausages!"

"PAH!" snorted another. "I'll make the sausages into sausage rolls. Then I'll feed them to a mangy old dog!"

Everyone, that is, except for Thorfinn, who nipped

swiftly back home to pick up some of Percy's bird food for the journey ahead.

It was difficult to find anything in the house as the whole place was crammed with his brothers' stuff. Wilfred had come back from Russia carrying a gigantic stuffed brown bear, which was squashed into the hallway, arms outstretched, jaws open. The bear was dressed in Sven's university scarf, mortarboard cap and cape, complete with skull and crossbones on the back. Thorfinn nearly tripped over Hagar's snowshoes and almost impaled himself on his brother's ice harpoon, which were littered on the stairs.

He eventually found the bird food, but on the way back out he noticed that his mother's wolf-skin slippers were missing from the shoe rack in the hall. Perhaps she'd been wearing them when she was taken.

Back at the longship, the crew hurried aboard. Oswald had to be lifted onto the boat using a pulley.

"Move it, you sloths!" he whined at the men hoisting the ropes.

"Oh, belt up or we'll drop you in the waves!" the men replied.

Velda wasn't part of the crew, but that had never

stopped her before. She hid in a barrel which was carried on board by the cook.

Percy flapped onto a mast to watch as everyone in the village clambered over each other to try and get aboard too.

"Oh, pick me! PICK ME!" they cried.

"I'll clobber 'em with my walking stick," shouted an old blind man with one leg.

"Hello there! Could someone help me?" cried Ergil the Wood-Whittler, who was STILL stuck inside the fishy barrel and had somehow managed to waddle to the shore.

“We already have a full crew,” growled Harald. “The rest of you can guard Indgar while we’re away.” He pointed at Erik the Ear-Masher’s son. “Olaf, you’re in charge!”

“By Odin’s beard!” muttered Oswald under his breath. “Who knows what we’ll find when we come back.”

The crowd still on the shore groaned. “AWWWW!”

Harald stepped up to the prow, gazing angrily ahead at the sea. His three eldest sons were at his side, tussling over the weapons they’d had to find for themselves without their mother’s help.

“That’s my sword!” shouted Hagar.

“No, Mum forged that one for me!” Wilfred snatched back the deadly weapon.

“Which one of you good-for-nothing fools has pinched my catapult?” roared Sven, kicking his brothers in the shins.

Thorfinn was the last to appear, packed and ready for the journey. “Let’s find poor Mother,” he said, patting Percy fondly.

Erik the Ear-Masher glowered at the crew. “Alright you pig-dogs! Cast off!”

CHAPTER 9

Harald and his crew pursued the raiders' boats out of the fjord and into the open sea.

"They outnumber us three ships to one," said Oswald.

"That's funny," said Thorfinn, drumming his fingers on his chin. "I was sure I saw four sails when they were ashore."

"Me too!" said Velda, clambering out of the barrel. "There were definitely four."

Erik raised his eyes to the heavens. "How in the name of Thor's breeches did this daft girl manage

to get aboard? She's bad luck! Her father was a ship-sinker!"

Velda growled at him then smirked. "Same way I always do – by outsmarting you."

"Three to one, you say, Oswald?" Harald said, ignoring their stowaway. "Huh! So what? We're Vikings. We laugh at such odds. I mean, look at the crew; they're loving it."

It was true. The Vikings relished the coming battle and were getting ready – sharpening swords, aiming spears, testing their shields. It didn't matter to them how many enemies they had to face.

"I vote we sail right in and board them at sea," said one lad, fizzing with excitement.

Oswald was the voice of reason. "Hmm... What if they have bowmen firing arrows, or a catapult, or marine infantry?"

"Who cares? We'll thrash 'em!"

"Let's split into three groups," said another. "We'll take a ship each."

"Hmmm... But we'll be weaker if we divide our forces," said Oswald.

"So what? We'll batter 'em!"

"YEAAAHHH!" chorused the Vikings. "So what?"

"We'll rip their gizzards!" cried one.

"We'll splatter their innards!" yelled another.

"We'll squash them with our big bottoms!" said a

man called Grut the Goat-Gobbler, who was famous for being the hungriest Viking in Norway. He did indeed have a very large bottom.

"YEA—" the others began, but stopped mid-chorus, screwing up their faces. "Na, you're on your own there, mate."

Thorfinn stepped into the middle of the debate, smiling and doffing his helmet. "Pardon me, dear sirs, but I have an absolutely fantastic idea. Why don't we just see where they're headed and follow them? I can keep track of them with my spyglass."

He looked through it at the raiders' ships and could see men playing pipes and others dancing. In fact, it looked like they were having a party.

"By Thor! Yes, that is a fantastic idea, Thorfinn," said Harald. "We'll follow them home, then attack them in their own village. We'll see how *they* like it. RAAAR."

"YEAAHHH!" cried the Vikings. "We'll burn their underpants – see how they like *that*!"

"Actually, I was going to suggest having a discussion with them," said Thorfinn. "There must be a better way to get Mum back than fighting."

"DISCUSSION! PAHH!" Erik the Ear-Masher snarled. "We're ferocious Vikings, boy! We don't discuss."

"YEAH! Stick your discussions!" shouted Sven.

"Discussions stink!" growled Wilfred

"Death to all discussions!" roared Hagar.

"We Vikings charge into action, we don't have discussions. Understand?" Harald glared at his youngest son, his twitchy eye twitching.

"Yes, I'd noticed," sighed Thorfinn.

CHAPTER 10

The afternoon wore on, and the sea winds chilled everyone to the bone.

"The ocean reminds me of the bleak, endless Russian plains," murmured a grim-faced Wilfred.

"Huh, what do you know about cold?" growled Hagar. "I had to camp on the Arctic ice pack."

"Oh, shut up you two," roared Sven. "The only thing you brought back from Russia, Wilfred, was a taste for cabbage, and that just makes you fart. As for you, Hagar, the cold has addled your already tiny brain."

Wilfred and Hagar rounded on their brother.

"Well, get you, Mr Smarty Pants, Mr 'I've been to Viking university'," said Wilfred.

"Yeh! You think you're cleverer than us, don't you?" said Hagar.

"I *am* cleverer than you," replied Sven.

"Hah! We've been fighting polar bears and Russian tribes. The toughest problem you faced was what to eat in the student canteen!" laughed Wilfred.

"Yeah, or which way round to wear that stupid black cap thingy," added Hagar.

Sven shoulder-shoved his two brothers to the ground, and they all started growling and challenging each other to a punch-up.

Harald grunted. "Save your fighting until we catch up with those raiders, boys!"

The crew huddled on deck, waiting for the return of the warm sun. Night fell, and by the following morning they found they were lagging even further behind the raiders' ships.

"Great Thor! We'll never catch up with them!" cried Harald.

"At this rate we'll lose sight of them within the hour," said Oswald.

Sure enough, the raiders' sails slipped below the horizon.

The chief assembled his four sons on the prow.

"You've been to university, Sven. You've done a kidnapping module. What's your advice?"

Sven gulped. "Oh, well, erm, the course didn't cover what to do if we got kidnapped. It mainly covered kidnapping other people."

"Fat lot of good you are," said Harald. He turned to Hagar. "And you? You're the tracking expert. What do you say?"

Hagar coughed and shifted in his furs. "When I was tracking polar bears the sea was all frozen and the bears left footprints. I don't suppose we're going anywhere frozen?"

"What a load of rubbish!" Harald dismissed him, turning to Wilfred. "And you? Any advice from your invasion of Russia?"

Wilfred looked sheepish. "You see, when I was in Russia there was no sea, just land everywhere—"

"Can I just stop you there," Harald said sharply.

"Yes, Father?" said Wilfred.

"Nothing. I just have to stop you. You're talking gibberish, like your brothers."

"Oh, don't be too hard on them, Father," said Thorfinn.

"What?!" snapped Harald.

"Remember, their mother has just been kidnapped. They're probably not thinking straight."

"Yeh! That's it!" replied Sven and Wilfred, and Hagar nodded too. "We miss our mum."

"Bah," Harald growled.

Thorfinn was dangling the small metal fish Oswald had given him in the air.

"What on earth are you up to?" Harald asked.

"It's a compass, Father. The fish is magnetic, so the nose always points north. Which means that those ships were heading south-west, away from Norway. I'd say they're heading for the Orkneys, or even Scotland."

Harald gazed out to sea, then back at his son. "By Odin, you're right, my boy." He turned to his crew. "Did you hear that everyone? They're heading for Scotland."

"Set a course for Scotland, you pig-dogs!" Velda screamed at the crew.

"Hoi!" cried Erik, pushing Velda out of the way. "Barking orders at the crew is my job! Clear off!" He cleared his throat. "Set a course for Scotland, you pig-dogs!"

CHAPTER 11

It was another two days before Thorfinn spotted land on the horizon. There was very little food left and everyone's bottoms had started to itch; they'd all been wearing the same underpants since they left Indgar.

"It's the north coast of Scotland," said Thorfinn, looking through his spyglass.

They skirted the coast for a bit, searching. Finally they came to a wide bay with a long, white, sandy beach.

"There they are!" cried someone, pointing to the sails of the raiders' boats, anchored next to a sleepy village.

“Excellent!” said Harald, rubbing his hands. “Now we have them.”

The Indgar longship beached with a huge jolt. Dozens of angry Vikings led by Harald and Erik leapt off screaming, and charged towards the dunes.

They were expecting a full-scale battle. They were expecting to be met with arrows, spears and a wall of shields.

And they were certainly being fired at. Erik got whacked square in the face with something squidgy – it was definitely not an arrow.

“YARRGH! It’s rotten fish! ” he cried, scraping a huge splat of brown goo from his cheek. “Vikings HATE fish!”

Volleys of putrid seafood were being launched at them from catapults beyond the dunes.

SPLAT! SPLAT! SPLAT! SPLATTTTT!

"Fiends!" cried Sven, batting the slimy missiles away with his shield. "Who fires rotten food at noble Viking warriors?"

"Cowards!" snarled Wilfred.

"Renegades!" roared Hagar.

Harald swiped at the fish with his sword, slicing them in half, and raved, "You devils! You devils!"

Velda parried the fish away with high kicks. "HI-YAAA!"

Oswald did the wise thing, pulling up his hood and hiding behind Erik's back.

Thorfinn was standing right at the back, so none of the fish reached him. In fact, he barely even noticed what was going on, but gazed up at the clear blue sky with Percy perched on his hand. "Isn't this a beautiful beach, dear Percy?"

The oil from the fish had made the beach very slippery. Harald's men slithered all over the place as they tried to charge over the dunes. They dropped their weapons and their legs flew out from under them.

Harald's Viking warriors soon turned into a heaving mass of arms and legs.

As they finally crested the dunes, Erik and Harald struggled to their feet and picked up their swords, ready to face their foes behind a wall of shields. But instead of a menacing army, they saw a bunch of people sitting around with their helmets and shoes off, watching and applauding.

"Nice landin' there, guys! Hope you enjoyed oor leftover fish."

There were men and women dancing about and others playing bagpipes. There were children playing about. They'd set up windbreaks and parasols. A few were munching sandwiches. One or two had even fired up a brazier and were having a barbecue.

"What is the meaning of this?" cried Harald, his eye twitching furiously at them.

"Surrender or die!" snarled Erik, spitting a fish tail out of his mouth.

A tall, bulgy-faced, red-haired man put down the chicken leg he was eating, wiped his hands with a napkin and stepped towards them.

"Ach, you win. We surrender, of course."

"You WHATTT?!" yelled Harald, insulted. He hated it when people surrendered, as it meant there would be no battle. And what made it worse, these people were Vikings, like them. "Vikings don't surrender!"

They were funny-looking Vikings though. They wore tartan along with their Viking helmets.

The tall man shrugged, then stretched out his hand and smiled. "I'm Gerry the Pie-Nosher. I'm the boss o' this mob here... Well, this rabble more like, ha ha!" He laughed.

But Harald was unamused. He slapped the man's hand away with his sword. "Vikings don't shake hands either. What kind of Vikings are you?"

"Scottish ones," replied Gerry.

CHAPTER 12

"Our granddads were like you lads," said Gerry. "They came from Norway. They conquered this bit o' Scotland. Then they decided tae settle here and farm the land. So we're half-Viking, half-Scottish."

Thorfinn appeared at his father's side, along with his three brothers. He doffed his helmet to the man and bowed. "Good morning, dear sir. And what a beautiful day."

Gerry bowed back. "Good morning to you as well. Ha, whit a polite wee laddie."

Harald bristled. "Will you STOP exchanging

pleasantries! Vikings don't do pleasantries!"

"Death to all pleasantries!" echoed a voice behind him.

"Well, you boys started it," Gerry replied, nodding at Thorfinn.

"He's not with us!" cried Erik, trying to push Thorfinn out of the way.

"Well, he is..." said Harald, pulling him back, "...and he isn't. Look, he's my son, that's all. I can't help it if he's a bit daft."

"And what sort of a Viking name is 'Pie-Nosher'?" said Erik. "What a rubbish name for a Viking chief!"

"Ha!" Gerry spluttered. "Somebody thought it up for a laugh."

Erik nearly choked. "A laugh? A LAUGH?!"

"Here," said Gerry, now munching on a rack of

barbecued ribs. "Ah'll introduce ye to ma pals."
He beckoned forward a bunch of men, all dressed in tartan like him. "This is Wullie the Stair-Runner-Upper. We send him tae take all oor messages, so he's forever runnin' aboot."

There was a gasp of horror from Harald and the other Vikings. And the names only got more ridiculous. "This is Hughie the Baldy-Heided, Ally the Garden-Gnome-Collector, Murdo the Chip-Eater and Ian the Shelf-Putter-Upper. He's brilliant at DIY."

Each name brought a larger gasp than before.

Harald nearly choked. "What... what sort of Viking names are those?"

Gerry shrugged. "Ah told ye, we're Scottish Vikings. We do everythin' for a laugh. It's the Scottish in us. That's why we came over the sea and raided your village."

"You raided our village... for a LAUGH?!" Harald's eyes were murderous now, and his cheeks flamed with fury.

Gerry tossed away the rack of ribs, which he'd stripped to the bone, then picked up a sandwich with a huge dripping hunk of meat inside it. He offered it to Harald and the men. "Goat burger anyone?"

Harald waved him away angrily.

Gerry shrugged and began chomping on it. "Aye, well, you know, everybody's fed up wi' the Norwegian Vikings, sailing over here and attackin' us. We thought it would be funny if we sailed over tae you fur a change."

The Vikings were blazing with fury. They were jumping around, yelling, "FUNNY?! A LAUGH?!"

"Well, as I did mention," said Thorfinn, "it didn't seem like much of a raid. See, it was all just a big joke."

"You're right, it wasn't much of a raid," said Erik. He went on, jabbing his finger at Gerry, "And that's another thing for *you* to be ashamed about."

"He's right," said Harald. "Your crew have a lot to learn about raiding."

Gerry shrugged. "You lot can't take a joke. You need to lighten up a bit."

"You're supposed to be Vikings, yet you didn't even bother to raze the village to the ground," said Erik.

"A bunch of children could do better!" said Harald.

"Ach, it was that pretty, with the mountains and the fjords and aw that," said Gerry. "It would've been a shame tae burn it doon. We thought it would be funnier to burn your underpants."

At the mere mention of the word 'underpants' the Vikings all scratched their bottoms, remembering how long they'd been wearing the same pair.

"And another thing," cried Erik. "You didn't even nick anything. We had loads of gold and you didn't even touch it."

"Ach, we don't need anything," said Gerry.

The Vikings tutted. "Dear, oh dear!"

"You Scottish Vikings, you should be ashamed," said Harald. "You've lost all your Viking spirit. OHH—" Harald stopped abruptly and dismissed Gerry with a wave of his hand. "Why am I even bothering to talk with you anyway. Now, where's my wife?"

Gerry looked confused. "Your wife?"

"Yes, my wife, the woman you kidnapped? Blonde hair, green eyes, ferocious temper. If you just give her back we'll be on our way."

"Eh, sorry, ah think there's been some mistake," said Gerry. "We don't have your wife."

CHAPTER 13

Gerry the Pie-Nosher turned to his friends to ask about Harald's missing wife. Then he slapped his forehead with the palm of his hand.

"There *was* a woman. We thought she was an escaped prisoner. She attacked us as we were heading back to oor boats. She gave us a real doing! She nicked one of oor longships and sailed off in it. We tried tae chase her, but she was too fast."

"A-ha!" said Thorfinn. "I was right – there *were* four ships."

Harald scratched his head. "I don't get it. If *you* don't

have her, and *we* don't have her, then who has her?"

"Pardon me, dear Father, but maybe *no one* has her," said Thorfinn.

"What do you mean, boy?"

"I think she's quite on her own. But if you'll bear with me, I can tell you where I think she's gone." Thorfinn opened his pouch and carefully unfolded the page his mum had ripped out of *The Daily Hatchet*. He pointed to the advert:

COME TO FLOTTERHEIM ICELANDIC SPA!

"Iceland?" said Harald, screwing up his face. "I don't think so. Why would she run off without telling us? And why would she want to 'relax'?"

“I hate to cause any upset,” replied Thorfinn, “but I think she was rather fed up.”

“Fed up? FED UP?” roared Harald.

“Vikings don’t get fed up,” said Sven.

“I mean, we have the best life in the world,” added Hagar.

“What’s not to like about the Viking life?” Wilfred joined in. “All the sailing about, the fighting, the burning and pillaging, the meat eating.”

“Yeah, sometimes all at once,” added Erik. “Eh, boys?”

"HUZZAH!" cried the entire Viking mob.

“Pardon me, I’m sorry to correct you,” said Thorfinn. “But Mother’s life is not that great.”

“What in Thor’s name are you talking about?” asked Harald.

Velda suddenly leapt between them, swishing her axe about. "Oi! How stupid are you lot?"

"Stupid?" cried Erik. "How dare this scrawny girl call me stupid!"

"She's calling you stupid," wheezed Oswald, "because you *are* stupid."

"Will you listen to Thorfinn for once in your miserable lives!" Velda's piercing eyes shot daggers at Harald and Thorfinn's brothers. "Freya doesn't get to do much of that fun Viking stuff. She spends most of her time cleaning up after you lot. When she's not repairing damage to the house, she's preparing the next meal or washing your massive underpants. You're all too blind to see it, you bunch of idiots. You deserve to get walloped." She turned to Thorfinn. "Oh, please let me wallop them, Thorfinn? Just a quick bash on the bonce, I promise!"

"No thanks, old friend," said Thorfinn, turning again to his father. "But Dad, Velda is right. Remember last week, for example, when Mother asked you not to break down the door for the fourth time running? Pardon me, but you just kicked it in anyway. And then you did it again, and again. Remember when she asked you for help carrying that elk to the harvest feast? You ignored her, and she put her back out by lifting it herself."

Harald rubbed his beard and there was a moment's silence, during which the only sounds to be heard were the lapping waves, and the munching and slurping as the Scottish Vikings tucked into a load of chargrilled venison.

Then Harald spoke again. "Ach! I can't believe she would run away and leave me over such nonsense!"

"Believe it!" replied Velda.

"She took her wolf-skin slippers when she left," said Thorfinn. "Now why would she do that unless she was planning to go somewhere relaxing?" He turned to Gerry. "Pardon me, dear sir, but would you please be so good as to tell me which way my mother's ship went when you left the fjord?"

"Aye, nae bother. She went aff to our right," said Gerry.

"That would be north-west, wouldn't it, to Iceland?"

Harald sighed, then got to his feet. "Well, what are you waiting for?" he yelled to his men. "Set sail for Iceland."

Erik protested, but Harald cast his twitchy eye at him. So Erik shrugged, then yelled at the men, "OK, you pig-dogs, back to the ship!"

The men grumbled and began climbing back aboard the longship. Thorfinn doffed his helmet to Gerry. "Good day, Mr Pie-Nosher!"

"Aye," said Gerry, now gnashing his way through a leg of lamb, "come back any time."

CHAPTER 14

The journey to Iceland took several days, during which Velda studied sea scrolls that had belonged to her father, Gunga the Navigator.

"Thorfinn, will you come and help me with my map?" She was struggling to hold it in the sea breeze.

"Why, of course, dear friend." Thorfinn helped

straighten it out and weigh it down with wooden blocks. "What does it show?"

"It's the whole northern ocean," said Velda. "And here..." she traced her finger along a line that ran the length of the map, "...is the route my father planned to take towards the New World in his ship, the *Night Blaze*." She sighed. "There's little chance of finding him now, I guess."

"There's always hope, dear friend." Thorfinn sat down on the deck and put his arm round Velda's shoulder. "How you must miss him."

"Mmm..." she said sadly. "Which is why it's so important that we find your mum."

Laughter boomed out behind them. It was Erik the Ear-Masher, who had been eavesdropping on their conversation. "Ha! Your father was the worst navigator we ever had."

Velda leapt to her feet. There was fire in her eyes. "You lot didn't appreciate him. He had loads of great ideas, like discovering the New World. He was going to call it Gungaland."

Erik laughed so hard he nearly threw up. "Gungaland? Shmungaland!"

Meanwhile Harald was staring gloomily out from the prow of the longship, surrounded by his sons.

Thorfinn climbed up on a barrel to pat his father's giant shoulder. "Oh, dear Dad, it's not your fault. You're a Viking; it's not in your nature to be

thoughtful." Percy fluttered onto Harald's other shoulder and patted it with his wing.

"What are you on about, boy?" Harald cried, pushing Percy away. He shook off his son's hand and ogled him like a deranged bear. "I'm going to Iceland to drag your mother back, whether she likes it or not."

"Yeh!" said Wilfred. "She should be grateful to have such a fearsome chief for a husband."

"Yeh!" agreed Sven. "And three great warrior sons."

"Yeh!" added Hagar. "She should be proud to clean up our mess."

Velda appeared at Thorfinn's side, her arms folded defiantly. "You can't just drag her back, you nitwits."

"What do you suggest we do then?" growled Harald.

"Pardon me, Father, but might I suggest you start by apologising?" said Thorfinn.

Harald took a sharp intake of breath at the mere mention of the despicable, un-Vikingy 'A' word.

"WHAATTT?!! APOLOGISE?!"

cried Harald.

"APOLOGISE?!" growled Sven, Hagar and Wilfred.

"Sometimes it helps to admit when we've been wrong," said Thorfinn.

Erik the Ear-Masher stepped in. He too was growling. "You're not going to take this, are you, Chief?"

Harald snarled – the fierce, angry snarl of a wounded animal. "Apologise? NO! I will not! Vikings DO NOT apologise!"

He barged past them all, then stopped and turned to Thorfinn. "And Viking wives DO NOT run off on spa breaks, get it?"

CHAPTER 15

At last, after many days of rolling seas and cold grey skies and itchy bottoms, the crew sighted the rugged coastline of Iceland. After another day Thorfinn spotted a sign through his spyglass. "There! Look!"

They beached the longship. Harald leapt onto the shore, his feet casting up a plume of sand. He bellowed, "Right, everyone stay put, apart from my four sons. We'll deal with this as a family."

"Pardon me, dear Father," said Thorfinn, gliding down a rope and landing with a puff of sand next to him, "but can Velda come too? She's good pals with Mother, and may be able to help."

"Fine," said Harald. Velda high-kicked with excitement as she back-flipped off the ship and somersaulted across the sand.

"I think I'll stay on board and rest my poor old tootsies. This icy weather is playing havoc with my chilblains," Oswald grumbled.

"Well, if the puny girl is coming," said Erik, landing right next to Velda and sending a spray of sand into her face, "then I'm coming too."

Percy fluttered onto Thorfinn's shoulder, and they set off marching along the beach. A few other longships were moored there, including one that looked very much like the raiders' boats. Thorfinn and Velda climbed aboard and unfurled the sail to reveal the raiders' skull and crossed-axes symbol.

"She's here!" cried Sven, throwing his mortarboard hat into the air.

"She must be!" added Wilfred, breaking into a comedy Russian dance.

"By Odin's hailstones!" cried Hagar, leaping into the air and clicking his heels.

They trekked on, past a number of shipwrecks. One of the wrecks was older than the others. The hull had sunk into the sand and the wood was bleached. A dragon figure, once polished bronze but now tinged with blue, lurched out from the masthead. Harald stopped and looked it over.

"Hang on, that ship looks familiar."

"Wait, that's one of ours!" said Erik.

Velda traced her fingers over the boat's name, now worn by the surf. "NIGHT B..." She yelped. "*Night Blaze*! It's the *Night Blaze*, my father's ship!"

"By Thor's beard, she's right," said Harald. "Old Gunga must have landed here! And he can't have gone much further without his boat."

"I wonder if he's still here?" said Thorfinn.

"Worse luck," barked Erik. "That old codger's all we need!"

Velda spat. "Don't you say that about my father!"

Harald took the furious girl by the shoulder and led her on. "Come on, let's take a look."

CHAPTER 16

The Vikings followed a path up from the beach and over a hill towards a bleak, rocky landscape. Here and there, geysers of hot water shot up from the ground. Beyond the rocks was a plain with a large steaming lagoon that was surrounded by a high fence. There were crowds of people inside, basking in the warm water.

“So this is the spa,” said Thorfinn. “What a wonderful place it looks.”

“C’mon, let’s climb over the fence,” said Sven.

“Let’s break it down,” said Wilfred.

“Let’s slash it with our axes!” said Hagar.

“No.” Harald pointed out the sentries and barking dogs patrolling the fence. “Better not if we want to find your mother.” A line of carts was dropping people off outside a large wooden fort. “That must be the reception. Let’s just use the front door.”

They made their way down to the fort, where they had to join a queue for the reception desk.

Erik protested. "This is ridiculous. We're Vikings, we don't queue!"

Harald silenced him with a look from his twitchy eye.

They eventually reached the front and were greeted by a man with slicked-back hair and a smooth voice. "Good day, gentlemen. Which day spa package would you prefer – bronze, silver or gold?"

Harald shrugged. "I don't care. We'll take the cheapest one."

"Pardon me, dear Father," said Thorfinn, "but the gold package includes a nice scalp massage."

"Gold *is* our best value package," said the man.

"Fine!" said Harald. "How much?"

"That will be forty gold pieces, sir," said the smarmy receptionist.

"WHATT?!" cried Erik, his face flushing with anger. "FORTY?! That's daylight robbery. And I'm a Viking; I should know."

"FINE!" said Harald. "Let's just get in, shall we?" He counted out his money.

The man smiled again. "Thank you, sir. Here are your tokens. Now, would you like to rent towels, slippers and robes for your visit?"

Hagar nearly choked. "Are you mad? Vikings don't wear robes and slippers!"

"Oh, plenty of them do, sir," replied the man. "We are a popular holiday destination for Vikings. It makes a nice change from all the burning and pillaging."

"No," said Harald. "We'll be fine as we are."

The man sucked sharply through his teeth. "You're not allowed in the lagoon area with normal clothes on, sir."

"Oh, please Dad," said Thorfinn. "I'd love a nice robe."

"Fine!" said Harald, again.

"That'll be another six gold pieces."

"WHATT?!" cried Erik. "I'm in the wrong business. C'mon, let's fight them!"

At which point a troupe of heavily armed and seriously muscular guards appeared out of nowhere to block the way.

"We can take these idiots!" Wilfred snarled.

"No!" said Harald, counting out more money, with a long sigh and a shake of the head.

"Well," said Thorfinn, "this is turning into an excellent day out."

They picked up their robes, slippers and towels and proceeded to the changing rooms. Erik, Harald and his boys cringed with embarrassment as they passed the line of guards.

"Oi! And leave your weapons here," said one of them.

Sven roared, "WHATT?! I'll slaughter you!"

More guards appeared, but Harald held Sven back. "No, we need to find my wife first."

"The chief's right," said Velda. "Stand down."

In the changing rooms there were three fist fights over lockers, four over towels, and another

two over slippers. Finally, they emerged enrobed in their luxurious white bathrobes. Erik still had his helmet on. "Well, I'm not taking this off at least. I've got my pride."

The Vikings had to queue up one final time to get through a gate, which was operated by a sad-looking elk. It moved forward to lift the barrier whenever someone put a token into the slot.

This riled Erik even more. "Another queue! Right, that's it!" He started to push his way through, but the guards appeared in front of him, blocking the way.

"You got a problem?" growled one of them.

Erik growled back. "C'mon, let's fight them!"

"We don't have our weapons," said Harald. "What are we going to do, flick them with our towels?!"

Erik seethed. "I want to speak to the manager!"

Thankfully Velda took control, herding the Vikings towards the gate and bundling them through one by one.

In the lagoon area at last, they looked to and fro, searching among the faces in the water, until Harald stopped suddenly and pointed to someone familiar at the far end of the lagoon.

CHAPTER 17

There she was, with her unmistakeable mane of long blonde hair and her piercing green eyes. Freya was lying back in the warm water, drinking from a big blue cocktail complete with cherries, pineapple, a tiny umbrella and a twirly straw.

"MUM!" cried Thorfinn's three brothers all at once. They marched over to her, with Harald leading the way.

"Freya!"

She looked up, saw Harald and her face fell. "Awww! What are you lot doing here? How did you find me?"

Thorfinn stepped out from behind his father's back and smiled. Freya grinned back at him and winked. "Ah, I might have known. He's the only one of you with enough brains."

"We've come to take you home," said Harald.

"Ha!" she laughed. "I'm not coming home. I'm having way too much fun."

"Dear Mother," said Thorfinn. "I don't suppose you'd mind if I joined you in the water?"

"Of course not, Thorfinn."

Thorfinn took off his robe and slipped into the steaming water beside her. "Ahhhh! Now that's very refreshing."

"Don't forget to try the mud," she said.

"Ooh yes, how could I forget." He scooped up

some whitish mud from the bank and smeared it all over his face, and Percy's too. "There you go, Percy. That will make you feel like a new pigeon."

Harald and the others watched all this with horror. Then Wilfred stepped forward, looking a bit like a scolded child. "Mum, what's all this about you not being happy?"

"Don't you like the Viking life?" said Sven.

"Why did you run away?" asked Hagar.

Freya simply sucked on her straw, draining her cocktail glass to the bottom. She tossed it away and shouted, "WAITER! Another fancy cocktail please!"

Beads of sweat appeared on Harald's brow. "Look, you're coming with us. Do I have to drag you back to the boat?"

Thorfinn's mother flexed her knuckles. "You can try, but I don't fancy your chances."

"Neither do I," yelled Velda, slipping into the water next to Freya. "And if you touch her you'll have two of us to contend with."

A small man with a teacherly look stepped towards them, flanked by guards. "Excuse me, is there a problem here? I'm the manager. Can I help you?"

There was something very familiar about his thin, squeaky voice. As soon as Velda heard it she sat bolt upright.

CHAPTER 18

The man took one look at Velda and gasped. "Velda? VELDA!"

She jumped out of the water and leapt into her father's arms. The two of them bounced around with joy.

"My little girl!" the man cried.

"I don't believe it! I found you! After all this time!" Velda shrieked.

"Gunga the Navigator!" said Erik. "Well I never."

Gunga put his daughter down and turned to Harald and the others. "It's about time you got here. Where have you been? Didn't you get my pigeon posts?"

Everyone looked at each other, then at Percy, who appeared to shrug his wings.

"No!" said Harald. "We didn't."

"Oh, I sent them south, so you should have got them."

"Pardon me, dear sir," said Thorfinn, "but Norway is east of here, not south."

"Oh, is it?" said Gunga, scratching his bald head.

"How did you end up in this awful place?" asked Harald.

"Well," said Gunga, "I was on my way to discover the New World, as you know, and I got shipwrecked here.

There was nothing to do, so I decided to build this holiday resort around the hot springs. Do you like it?"

Erik glowered at him. "As a matter of fact, NO!"

"See!" said Velda. "I kept telling you I'd find my dad one day. I kept telling you he had great ideas, and you never believed me."

"You call this slime-pit a great idea?" said Erik.

"I had big plans for the place. I was about to build a casino over there, but there's no point now."

"But why not, Mr Navigator?" asked Thorfinn.

"Because you've come to get me." He squeezed his daughter's hand. "And we're going home. Isn't that right, Velda?"

"You bet we are, Dad!" They started walking towards the turnstile.

"Wait!" said Harald, turning back to his wife. Freya was sipping from a new cocktail, a bright pink one with half a banana hanging off the side of the glass. "Freya, I... I..."

Erik glared. "You're not going to say what I think you're going to say, are you?"

"I... ap—" Harald struggled to get the words out. "I... ap—"

"Vikings don't apologise!" snapped Erik.

Harald snarled at Erik. "Butt out, Ear-Masher!"

Erik shrank back.

Harald stiffened, then sank to his knees. "Look, I'm sorry. I've been a blind fool!"

Thorfinn's three brothers followed their father's lead, slumping down behind him. "We're sorry too, Mum."

"Will you please just come home?" asked Harald.

Thorfinn's mother smiled. "Well, since you put it *sooo* nicely." She stepped out of the water and put on her robe. "C'mon then, Thorfinn."

Thorfinn took her hand and smiled. "Yes, Mum, let's."

Freya and Thorfinn led the way back to the ship.

CHAPTER 19

"SHHHHHHHHHH!"

Breakfast time in any Viking house was a messy business, but in the house of Harald the Skull-Splitter, the famous Viking chief, it was different now – a calm, quiet, civilised affair.

Wilfred was wearing an apron and frying sausages over the hearth, Sven was laying the table, and Hagar was milking the cow outside. Harald was sitting at the head of the table reading *The Daily Hatchet* newspaper. Beside him sat Thorfinn, his napkin, eggcup, knife and spoon set out in front of him.

Thorfinn's mother entered, wearing a bearskin robe. Harald stood up, somewhat sheepishly for a ferocious Viking chief.

"Ahem... Morning."

"Good morning everyone," said Freya.

"The sausages will be ready in a minute, Mother," said Wilfred.

"The table is set," declared Sven.

"I'M NEARLY FINISHED MILKING THE COW!" called Hagar from outside.

Freya sat down next to Thorfinn and flicked open her napkin. "Wonderful."

"How are you enjoying being back?" asked Thorfinn.

"I'm tickled pink," she said, with a smile. "What would I do without you, Thorfinn?"

"And what would we do without you, Mother? Welcome home."

THE END

DAVID MACPHAIL left home at eighteen to travel the world and have adventures. After working as a chicken wrangler, a ghost-tour guide and a waiter on a tropical island, he now has the sensible job of writing about yetis and Vikings. At home in Perthshire, Scotland, he exists on a diet of cream buns and zombie movies.

RICHARD MORGAN was born and raised by goblins on the Yorkshire moors. After running away to New Zealand to play with yachts and paint backgrounds for Disney TV he returned to the UK to write and illustrate children's books. He now lives in Cambridge, England, and has a family of goblins of his own.

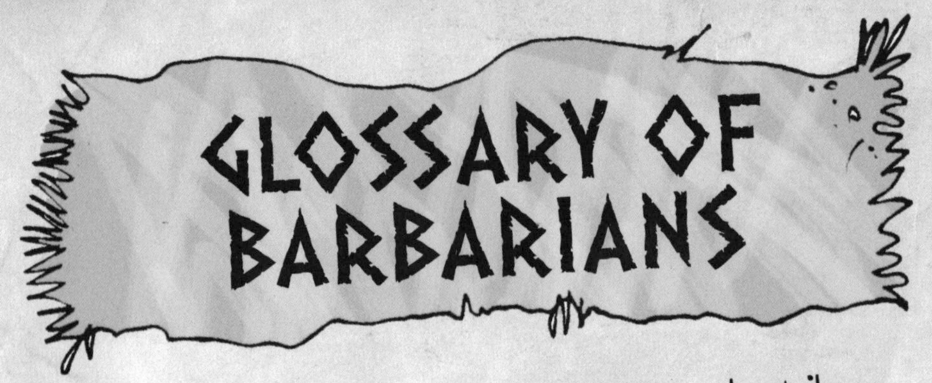

During the Dark Ages, Europe was overrun by tribes of BARBARIAN raiders. The Vikings were just one of these tribes.

THE NORMANS

They were originally Vikings too, but they decided to call themselves 'The Normans' to lull their enemies into a false sense of security. After all, who could be terrified of someone called 'Norman'? But it was all a trick. They landed in France claiming to be on a caravanning holiday. They tricked the natives and nicked their land, which later became known as 'Normandy'. William the Conqueror, the chief Norman, successfully invaded England in 1066. He was so fat that after he died his body EXPLODED in its coffin.

THE FRANKS

They were not all called Frank either – though some of them might have been. I don't know, I wasn't there! They made a fortune out of buying and selling used carts, after which they gave their name to France.

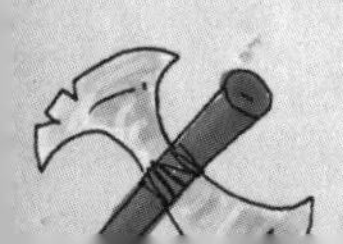

THE GOTHS

Were a dark-haired tribe from Germany who wore lots of black eyeliner. They rampaged through Europe writing bad poetry and complaining that their parents just didn't understand them.

THE VANDALS

No one seems to know where they came from, but they toured the whole of Europe sacking, looting and spray-painting graffiti. They gave their name to the word 'vandalism'.

THE COSSACKS

They emerged from darkest Russia wearing bearskin hats and doing funny dances. At first people laughed, until they whipped out their great curved swords, called 'scimitars'.

THE PICTS

Were a strange legendary tribe shrouded in the dark mists of ancient Scotland. They charged into battle stark naked, wearing only blue paint. The Romans were so terrified of the Picts, they built Hadrian's Wall to keep them out.

THE HUNS

They started off as a medieval boy band, performing dance routines for legions of fans all around Europe. Then they got too old and the gigs dried up, so they turned to pillaging instead to pay for their pop-star lifestyle.

*DISCLAIMER – Some of these facts are not entirely accurate.

VIKING ANAGRAMS

As usual Thorfinn's brothers are in a muddle. Can you help them untangle these sentences?

1. ehTy nurdeb ruo seaundptnr!
2. yB idnO's barde!
3. lWl'e ipr etirh zzaigsrd!
4. eSt csorue ofr colnadtS, oyu ipg-dsog!
5. !iO owH piudst ear uoy tol?
6. kisVgni OD NTO gaooepsli!
7. kaTe taht, iecnchk ibnar!
8. eW hdouls lal akte rntsu ta odnig het okurhowse.

ANSWERS:

1. They burned our underpants! **2.** By Odin's beard!
3. We'll rip their gizzards! **4.** Set course for Scotland, you pig-dogs!
5. Oi! How stupid are you lot? **6.** Vikings DO NOT apologise!
7. Take that, chicken brain! **8.** We should all take turns at doing the housework.

MISSING MUM MAZE

Can you dodge Gerry's rotten fish and help Thorfinn find his mum?

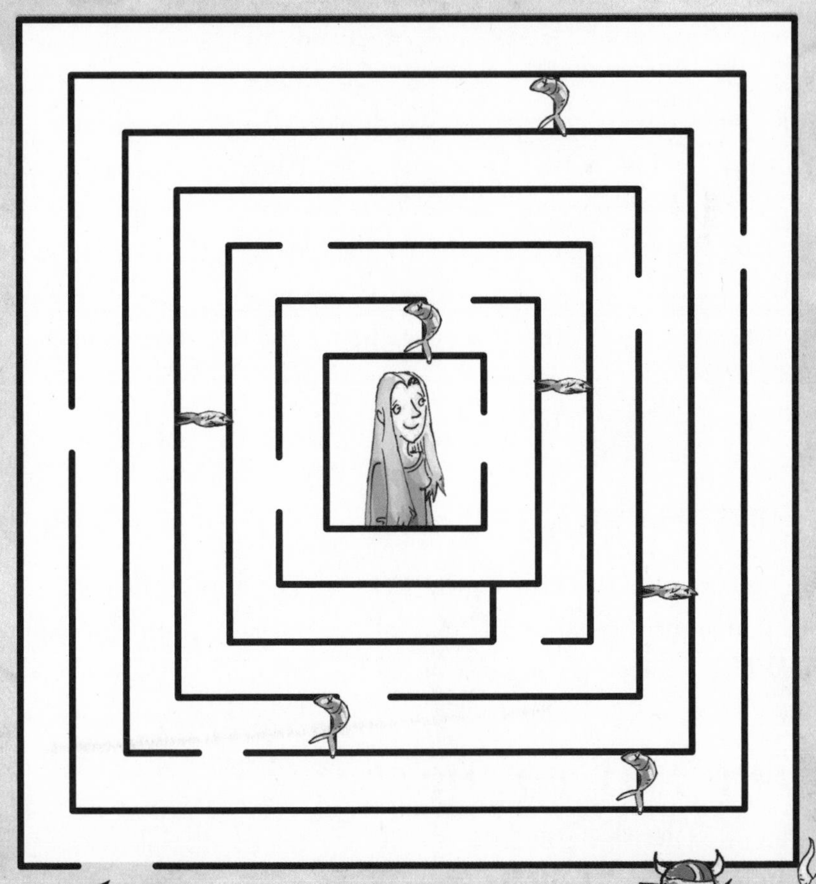

Start here!

PERCY THE PIGEON POST

EST. 799AD | ODINSDAY 18TH FEBRUARY | PRICE: ONE FRONT TOOTH

SKULL-SPLITTING NEWS

In what will forever be known as the Awful Invasion the Scots have narrowly missed being invaded by a band of maurauding Vikings, led by the fearsome Chief of Indgar, Harald the Skull-Splitter.

SPORTING HEADLINES

It is the weekend of the annual Gruesome Games. Word on the beach is that Thorfinn and his motley team have to save their village from the clutches of Magnus the Bone-Breaker. Odds are on for a new Chief of Indgar by Monday.

FOULSOME FOOD

It's all about Le Poisson (that's FISH to you boneheads). The King of Norway is on his way to Indgar and he expects a most Disgusting Feast. But there's a poisoner at large and the heat is on in the kitchen...

TORTUROUS TRAVEL

Early booking is essential to visit the Rotten Scots' most famous prisoner (that's Thorfinn) at Castle Red Wolf. Hurry – he may be rescued at any moment!

LOST AND NOT FOUND

A massive hoard of Terrible Treasure stolen from the pesky Scots has mysteriously vanished. Large reward promised for information leading to its recovery.

MISSING PERSONS

The Raging Raiders are prime suspects in the kidnapping of one fed-up, goat-carrying Viking mum. Please report any sightings to Chief Harald the Skull-Splitter.